Simply Weird

Simply Weird

The (fake) History of Weird Comics Incorporated,
A (fake) Comic Book Company

WILLIAM ROBERT WEBB III

authorHOUSE®

AuthorHouse™
1663 Liberty Drive
Bloomington, IN 47403
www.authorhouse.com
Phone: 1-800-839-8640

Published by AuthorHouse   09/17/2012

ISBN: 978-1-4634-2942-3 (sc)
ISBN: 978-1-4634-2941-6 (hc)
ISBN: 978-1-4634-2940-9 (e)

Library of Congress Control Number: 2011911674

For My Mother
Barbara Ann Webb

Who supported my interest in comics as a child and felt that reading (even if it were comics) was a very good way to spend my time as a child. Without her support of my love of comics I doubt this book would exist at all.

Also for My Father
William Robert Webb II AKA Bill Webb

For being a good dad and for his sense of humor.

And Most of all For My Late Grandmother
Edith Louise Zimmerly

The most caring, loving and generous person I have ever met. She was a Talented Poet who in her time was instrumental in fostering my creativity and giving me the push I needed as a writer.

DISCLAIMER:

The following despite being written like a nonfiction book is completely fictional. Also while this book does mention some actual people and historical events this book is completely fictional.

Trust me this is not real! Not at all!

. . . again this is completely fictional.

CONTENTS

Chapter 1

Pulps and the precursors to the peculiar history of Weird Comics Inc.

Weird Comics Inc. has a fairly peculiar history and its beginnings come from an odd series of events. To truly appreciate its formation one must look at a time before its creation/formation. One must look back at the career of Waldo Richard Winecrest II, whose publishing company Industrial Pulps was the parent company of Weird Comics Incorporated.

Waldo was born in London, England and not much else is known about his life before moving to the United States. Even family Members didn't really know when he was even born. Waldo Richards Winecrest IV (or Dicky Winecrest as he is most commonly known as) once said to me that he had, "asked my father when my grandfather was born. He then shrugged and told me he had no clue. Obviously I was pretty shocked to hear that."

The only bit of information that is known about Waldo is that during his years in London he worked at a company that published Penny Dreadfuls. It is said that Waldo wanted a change of scenery and wanted to jump into the blossoming American Pulp Market. So according to Elis Island records Waldo reached America's shores on the date of June 2nd 1924.

Some of Waldo's early dealings in New York are as much in the shadows as his days in London. Seemingly overnight Waldo formed Industrial Pulps which happened to published several pulp magazines in several genres. There were such titles as the Hard Boiled magazine "Private Dicks", the Science Fiction magazine "Tales of Uranus" and a horror magazine "The Gapping Horror" just to name a few.

Many happened to be puzzled with the fact that Winecrest a British immigrant could make such a quick and swift ascent into the business of Pulp magazines. This has led to much speculation and rumors. Many (then and now) hypothesized that the mob may have had some involvement with helping Waldo get the money needed to quickly expand Industrial Pulps. The thing though is that there is no solid evidence either way.

Dicky Winecrest's own take is that his grandfather must have, "gotten some money through an inheritance or something. I really doubt my grandfather was involved with the mob."

Never the less Waldo was riding high off of the success of Industrial Pulps and was seen as a very eligible bachelor at the time. He became legendary for his womanizing but he would soon settle down and leave his tomcat days behind him focusing mostly on business.

On July 7th 1925 Waldo would become a family man when he married a woman named Jane Dodson whom he had met through mutual friends. Their first and only child was born on January 14th 1926 named Waldo Richard Winecrest III (who was referred to as Richard by everyone he had known except Waldo). Waldo was somewhat disappointed in Richard as a son to say the least. Waldo would often refer to Richard as "That Git".

Commenting on the relationship between his father and grandfather Dicky Winecrest has said, "Sadly my Grandfather saw my father as some sort of disappointment. I never understood why and neither did my father. It was just a very bizarre relationship.

"My Grandfather once said that his disappointment in my father led to him deciding to not have any other children because of how much a disappointment my father was to him.

"I guess the fact my dad wasn't an athletic type of person didn't help since my Grandfather did want an athletic son. It also didn't help that my father would misunderstand some of the British colloquialisms that my Grandfather would use.

"Besides that there was also the fact that my father was an eccentric child who grew up into a very eccentric man. Now that I think about it those are probably some of the reasons my Grandfather was disappointed. Still those are pretty stupid reasons to hate your own son."

A few of the eccentricities that Richard would express during his childhood included (but not limited to) running around the house wearing his mother's bonnet, pacing in his room in a circle for hours while talking to himself and the fact that he demanded that cheese not be in his presence. These would usually anger his father who would stew in silence about his son's unusual behavior.

Most of these mentioned eccentricities would fall by the waist side over time while other eccentricities would take their place. One eccentricity from childhood that would follow Richard into adulthood would be pacing and talking to himself. He'd use as a method to come up with comic book stories as an adult.

While growing up Richard was an avid reader of Pulp Magazines including many that were published by his own father. Richard also happened to appreciate what would be considered more cultured reading. Along with his beloved Pulps he would read the likes of William Faulkner, Nikolai Gogol, James Joyce, Franz Kafka, Andre Breton, Albert Camus and Charles Maturin. Still his favorite author was Pulp writer H.P. Lovecraft. In Richard's eyes there was no high art and not low art, there was just the act of expression.

Richard also started reading newspaper comic strips around the age of twelve. The blend of the visual with the written word fascinated Richard. He was particularly fond of Alex Raymond's Flash Gordon and George Herriman's Krazy Kat.

During this time a new medium would come to the forefront. A medium that combined two of Richard's loves Pulp Magazines and newspaper comic strips. Of course this new medium would be called the comic book. With this new medium called comic books came a new sort of hero along with it. It would lead to the birth of the superhero.

Chapter 2

The Birth of Weird Comics Inc. and its rise
to prominence

aldo did not think much of his son so he wanted Richard out of his house by the time Richard was eighteen. So Waldo paid the amount of money needed to put Richard in and keep him in college. During his time in college Richard would meet his future wife June Day.

After a whirlwind courtship June found out she was pregnant. Waldo immediately demanded that Richard not only marry June but drop out of school and get a job. The problem then became that Richard wanted to work at Industrial Pulps. Waldo refused to give his son a job at Industrial Pulps on the ground that he didn't want to see his son's face on an everyday basis.

A deal was struck between father and son. The deal would be that Richard would be the head of a new division of Industrial Pulps that would specialize in comics. Richard would serve as Head Writer and Editor in Chief. The new comic book division of Industrial Pulps would be held in a different building than the one that Industrial Pulps was run out of. This was done so that Waldo would not have to see Richard a stipulation that was very important to Waldo.

With those series of events set in motion Richard and June would get married on January 15th 1946 (the day after Richard's twentieth birthday). While Richards was setting ground over the next couple of months his son Waldo Richard Winecrest IV[1] was born on July 7th 1946 (oddly enough on his grandparents wedding anniversary). The happiness of these two even would be overshadowed by the difficulty Richard was going through trying to get his upstart comic company off the ground.

---

1   Named Dicky so as not to be confused with either his father or grandfather.

Richard had very little experience in publishing except for working part time as a courier at Industrial Pulps during his High school days. Besides that he also had a handful of short stories published in some of the Pulp Magazines published by Industrial Pulps. This didn't matter to Waldo who honestly didn't care if anything was actually published. He only cared that his son would stay out of his hair. While most of Waldo's colleagues thought this reasoning was insane and financially irresponsible they kept their opinions to themselves (at the time).

Most of Richard's problems came from his inability to hire anyone to work for the fledgling comic company that at the time was simply called Weird Comics[2]. Sometime in around August Richard would hire the man that would help jumpstart the process that would finally get the company off the ground. That man was Phil Hardy, a veteran editor of several Pulp Magazines and a handful of comics. He left the business originally to join the army during World War II but when he came back from Europe he couldn't find a job.

Hardy would describe his working at Weird Comics as, "reaching for the bottom of the barrel. A low point but, the only other jobs I could find were low paying at the time. Weird Comics was the only place I could work at and make enough to live off of. Still it was humiliating working there but like I said it was better than making no money."

As assistant editor Hardy was able to bring in freelance artists. He was also able to find people to fill up all the positions at Weird Comics that Richard couldn't get filled. Hardy was a miracle worker who was about to take the business side and managerial side while Richard focused on the creative side.

---

2   The offices of Weird Comics had been occupied by Richard alone for
     nearly eight months. This would end in august.

Most would agree with this saying that beyond complete editorial control over the content being published at Weird Comics Richard paid no attention to the business side of things. Anything not directly involving the content of the comics was handled by Hardy.

Hardy thought this was best since according to him, "Richard would make people uneasy. He was kinda out there. He'd have this Salvador Dali type of moustache and a tiny pointy beard on his chin. Y'know like whatcha'd call a goatee.

"He was harmless but most people were afraid of him. Well except the creative guys like the artists and the few writers we had. Wait scratch that last part there was only one writer and that was Richard.

"I honestly think that the two things he liked the most at work was writing and hanging out with the artists. But he seriously scared everyone else."

With Weird Comics finally getting on track there was one speed bump that got in the way of its launch. That speed bump was Waldo Winecrest. Up until that point Waldo had completely ignored the comics division until he looked over the comics that were to be launched. A misunderstanding would almost completely derail the launch.

As Phil Hardy put it, "Richard's old man thought Richard wouldn't get any comics published. He just thought of it as a money hole so that Richard would stay away from him. Richard showed him wrong."

Though what distressed Waldo the most wasn't that the comics were to be published but was the name of the company and its logo. The Logo for Weird comics was simply its initials within a circle (WC). Waldo had mistakenly thought that his son had named his comic book company Water Closet.[3] With that Waldo would for the first and only time demand Richard make an editorial change. Richard would comply

---

3   It is a European term for restroom which is usually shortened to WC.

and change the name of the company Weird Comics Incorporated (shortened to WCI when referenced by most fans) which would remain its name throughout its storied history.

Since the print run had already been made Richard and many other employees of WCI had to manually write the letter I after the WC logo on the original run of comics published. Many hours were spent putting the letter on the comics at Waldo's request. A small portion of comics that made it to newsstands didn't have the letter I written after the WC logo. Those are now collector's items.

During this time Richard quickly came up with many characters and stories to populate the comics published by WCI. One of the first successes was a comic called Claws Son of Santa, a Christmas themed Superhero with retractable claws (made of candy canes) who happened to be the son of Santa Claus. The inspiration for the character somewhat came from a misunderstanding between Richard and Waldo when Richard was a child.

Waldo being British would always refer to Santa Claus as Father Christmas. As a young boy Richard always thought this meant that Santa was someone's actual father. Richard would not see how silly this was until he was an adult but the whole thing stuck with him.

Richard put a lot of his personal experience with his father as inspiration for the relationship between Claws and Santa. Claws was the superhero son of Santa Claus who like Richard was considered a disappointment by his father. In the character of Claws he found a much needed catharsis. He also found that while it was an odd idea it was one that struck a chord with readers much to the befuddlement to all who worked at WCI except Richard.

Phil Hardy would remark that, "We all thought it was too crazy an idea to appeal to kids. In the end we were all wrong. The comic sold like hot cakes. It surprised the hell out of all of us except Richard. It was like he had a golden touch or something."

With the success of Claws led to Richard being able to essentially write whatever he wanted to. No one would question his decisions. No idea was too crazy to print because of the success of Claws.

Besides several art classes in High school and College Richard had no art experience. Despite this he wanted to not only write but also draw a comic to be published by WCI. He wanted to draw and write a serialized comic within the Anthology comic Whole Lotta Comics.

Many wanted to say no since Richard was very limited in his drawing ability and was also a slow illustrator. On account of the success of Claws people said nothing. Richard was such a slow artist that it took him a whole month to complete one comic page. It wasn't very well drawn either.

Richard decided not to illustrate ever again but he did publish the completed page as a teaser for a Character to be published by WCI. Richard decided that he would get the (in his opinion) best freelancer working at WCI's. That artist that he chose was Leo Spitz.

Leo Spitz was born Leo Spitzleiberkurtzowoskiberg[4] in the Polish Village of Bebla in 1920.[5] His family left Poland for America in 1923 according to Elis Island records. He grew up poor in New York's Lower

---

4   There has been debate over why Spitz shortened his name. Some believe he did so to have a less "ethnic" sounding name but Spitz always vehemently denied this. He would also say that Spitz sounded more like a comic book artist's name. He also always felt that his birth name was too long. Interestingly there is also some debate as to whether or not Leo Spitzleiberkurtzowoskiberg was his real birth name. Still the Spitz family has always claimed that Spitzleiberkurtzowoskiberg was always his birth name

5   Not the exact year since there are no records but is commonly considered the most likely year.

East Side. To pass the time he's drew pictures and read newspaper comic strips. His favorite comic strips were Windsor McKay's Little Nemo in Slumberland and George Herriman's Krazy Kat. Young Leo admired the work of McKay and Herriman. Young Leo wished to become a comic strip illustrator. He felt that was the only way he could make something out of himself.

Richard had sent Phil Hardy to approach Leo with the job. This entailed giving Spitz a copy of the teaser that Richard had drawn along with a full script to be illustrated for an upcoming issue of Whole Lotta Comics. He looked at the title and was puzzled. Koltar the Mighty Immortal was the title character who happened to be a superhero.

Spitz didn't know what to say. He liked his current gig as artist on WCI teen comedy comic Tommy Pulls a Boner.[6] The comic in which the lead character Tommy Goodeboy would get into mischief while screwing up ("pulling many a boners"). Tommy was well known for his big ears and bow tie. The comic took allot of Spitz's time and he was worried he couldn't work on both comics. He was assured that each story would be no longer than ten pages. Spitz then reconsidered things and thought he could work on both comics.

Before Spitz made his final decision to work on Koltar he wanted to read the original teaser and the full comic book script. He didn't want to get stuck with something he wouldn't want to work on. He liked what he read because of its uniqueness and he was off to work on Koltar the Might Immoral.

The story of Koltar the Mighty Immortal was that of a brash scientist at the end of time who wanted to try and prevent the end of the universe. In an attempt to stall the destruction of the universe

---

6   During this time in history pulling a Boner meant screwing up or causing mischief.

he creates a machine. That machine doesn't stop the end of the universe but instead puts the scientist known as Koltar back to the 20th century.

There he discovers that the process of time travel has made him indestructible and there go has become completely immortal. After finding a superhero comic, Koltar decides to fashion a blue costume and becomes a superhero. He christens himself The Mighty Immortal. All of this was found within the one page teaser that Richard had illustrated.

The types of villains that Koltar would fight were also unique. Instead of colorful costumed criminals Koltar fought bizarre creature that seemed as if they came out the brain of Lovecraft. They were Eldritch Abominations with tentacles and misshapen bodies that would sometimes disguise themselves as humans (mostly as gangster but a couple of them were colorfully costumed supervillains). These were things that Leo wouldn't have had the opportunity to draw on a silly little teen comedy comic. After the success of Koltar the comic was turned into a short lived movie serial. It was surprisingly faithful to the comics but very few remember the it.

A very rough design of Koltar the Mighy Immortal done by Richard Winecrest.

Something else that came from this collaboration would be a close friendship between Richard and Leo. So close that their families would also become as close. To quote Dicky Winecrest, "Leo was my dad's best friend. With that in mind it was no surprise our families did a lot together. If the Winecrests had a family get together then the Spitzs wouldn't be far behind or vice versa."

During this time Leo would end up becoming Art Director at WCI. He would remain in that post until his untimely death in 1954. Still things were looking up for WCI with all its movers and shakers in place. They sold a few comics on the way too. Richard would be always hard at work working on new characters.

A flood of new characters came into existence. So many characters appeared that Richard decided to introduce a superhero team. He would call it The Legion Society of Protectors. Phil Hardy voiced the opinion that he felt the name should be changed. He felt that the name was too awkward and that it would confuse kids.

Hardy would later say, "I honestly tried to convince him to choose a simpler name. He wouldn't have it. So I decided to just not worry about it."

The LSP (as it was nicknamed by those around the offices) had many odd superheroes. These included Starry Knight a knight themed hero who wielded the mighty Excalibur while having a star on his chest. There was also American Man, a surprisingly generic patriotic superhero. Then there was Moonchild a girl sidekick with vague mystical powers whose origins would not be revealed until decades later. Then there was the masked detective known by the name The Grey Apparition. Then there was The Mark a man whose mask was simply a mask with a question mark on it.[7] Lastly there was The Boot, a hero whose main superpower was that he had a gigantic boot that gave him super kicking powers. More characters were intended to be added to the team but it didn't last more than a couple of issues.

The Legion Society of Protectors completely failed in the marketplace. Many copies of the first issue were returned to WCI. Phil Hardy's assessment of the title was right. The name was just too damn confusing for kids. It didn't help that none of the superheroes appeared on any of the covers during the comics short run. Only the villains were feature on the cover with and ominous look on their face with no context what so ever.

The title would be canceled immediately but two more issues made it to the newsstands (which were immediately returned) and two more unpublished issues.[8] There wouldn't be another attempt at reviving the book until the 1970's (though the characters would appear sporadically through the years in other comics and Moonchild would get an ongoing comic feature in the 1960's). The only kid who seemed to like The LSP was Dicky Winecrest who found copies of the comic in the Winecrest's attic.

Besides this one hiccup everything would work smoothly at WCI for the rest of the decade. Things were fine until the looming 1950's came on the horizon. Tastes changed and a man named Wertham

---

7   Many wondered how he was able to see through the mask but that was beside the point when the character was dropped after one issue never to be heard from again. He is probably the most obscure character in WCI's catalogue.

8   The two unpublished issues would be published during the 1970's revival of The Legion Society of Protectors then published simply as The LSP.

would change comics forever. Along this that came much hardship and tragedy as the 50's came along. WCI would have problems as a result of all those events happening during that decade. Still while they would come back out of the ashes like a phoenix.

Chapter 3

WCI survives being at the brink and then feels the Wrath of Wertham and the comic code and then Rises from the Ashes

Weird Comics Inc. came in the later end of the initial superhero trend in comics and still flourished while other superhero comics died off. That was until 1951 when things had gotten so bad with superhero trend of comics that Richard Winecrest was forced to cancel all of WCI's superhero comics.

This left only the teen comedy comic Tommy Pulls a Boner and the newly launched science fiction comic Science By a Different Name as the only comics published by WCI at the time. By this time the only superhero still being published was Koltar the Mighty Immortal who had just been relegated to being a ten page backup in Science By a Different Name.

With the large cancelation of nearly the whole line of comics published by WCI led to Richard being forced to turn down dozens of freelance artists. The only artist left on WCI's payroll was Leo Spitz who did all the art for Tommy Pulls a boner and Science of a Different Name.

After only a couple of months Leo felt he was spread too thin. He would soon decide to bring his fourteen year old son Stan on as his ghost artist on the comic Tommy Pulls a Boner.

Stan would also draw at least one story in Science of a Different Name an issue. Stan would recall that he, "wasn't paid anything but it was an important learning experience nonetheless. I don't think I would be nearly as good an artist if I hadn't worked on those comics at that time in my life. It was a great way to start off my career."

Though things were bleak at WCI Richard was planning for WCI to have a big comeback. He noticed that the comic Science by a Different name was doing very well over its two years of publication. He also noticed the new trend of horror and science fiction comics that he saw becoming successful at other companies. He saw the direction he needed to steer the company towards.

He would make many changes such as turning Tommy Has a Boner into a science fiction comic called Tommy in Space. He would also revive some of his father's long forgotten Pulp horror magazine The Gapping Horror as a comic book.

Richard also launched two new science fiction comic books. Their names where Science to Amaze and Science Monsters (a formulaic comic staring giant monsters created by the result of science going wrong). There was also a horror/science fiction fused comic titled Tales of Space Horror.

The overhaul of WCI's whole line of comics started in February of 1952 (nearly a year since Richard was forced to cancel all of WCI's comics except for two). The new Changes led to a new surge in sales at the lagging company. While not as successful as they had been in their superhero days WCI was doing gangbusters in comparison to when they were several years before.

Things had gotten so good that Richard decided to launch a couple of more comics in the vein of the new Sci Fi and Horror comics. One of the new comics was a revival of Claws Son of Santa. Claws having retired as a superhero had become a space cowboy who fought aliens. Another comic launched in the wake of WCI's new success was a horror series called Vamps about a group of sexy vampires. While the new version of Claws Son of Santa was successful Vamps was very unsuccessful.

Still things seemed to be getting better at WCI and things would be that way for a couple of years before things would get bad again. Fredrick Wertham was making waves with his book

Seduction of the Innocent. In the book Wertham posited that many comic books led the youth of America to become hoodlums and criminals. The book led to a senate subcommittee on comic books.

A hysteria over the content found in comic books and their effect on children soon followed. The rampant paranoia led to an atmosphere not unlike the reaction towards the debut of Rock and Roll soon after the hysteria of comic books had died down. In the midst of all this paranoia and hysteria WCI had a tragic event happen.

On a breezy day in 1954 Richard Winecrest, Waldo Winecrest and Leo Spitz went for a drive. They were going to go to a meeting place where Waldo was planning on announcing his retirement as head of Industrial Pulps. He was also planning on making Richard head of Industrial Pulps.[9] The car crashed before they could reach their destination.

The carnage created by the crash killed both Waldo and Leo. Richard would survive but would live with survivor's guilt for the rest of his life. It would haunt him until the day that he would die. Many would say that Richard could never be the same.

Dicky would say, "My father had finally started to have a good relationship with my grandfather. My grandfather even trusted my dad with taking over Industrial Pulps and then he was taken away from him. On top of that he also lost his best friend. On the same day he lost his father he also lost Leo. Leo, who was his best friend.

"To say that dad was depressed at the time would be an understatement. On top of all this Wertham was spewing his nonsense

---

9   While he still didn't like his son he did look at the success of WCI as a good reason to hand Industrial Pulps over to Richard.

that would lead to major changes in the comic book industry. The fact that this all happened to coincided with each other made things even more worse than they could have been.

"My father had a hole in his heart and he had to take over Industrial Pulps. On top of that he had to find someone to fill Leo's position as Art Director at WCI. He also had to get used to changes in the industry while he was still grieving. That was a lot to have on his plate. I'm surprised my father didn't go completely off the rails or insane."

Richard would take over Industrial Pulps and quickly replace Leo with Leo's son Stan. Stan not only took over his dad's assignments but many noticed that he was noticeably more gifted as an artist than his father was. Well just don't try and tell Leo that.

Leo would react to those saying his art was better than his dad by saying, "That's a bunch of shit. My father was a great storyteller and a great draftsman. I honestly feel I don't at all hold a candle to my dear departed father. If anyone comes close to his greatness it is my sister Sally."

Things seemed to smooth over at least until the comic book code came along[10]. The code was there in an attempt to sanitize comics and debuted right after Richard got WCI back on track. It would make demands on toning down violence and mandating what words could be used in titles of comics among other demands.

Richard had many battles with the code and he lost many of them. After two years of it Richard was fed up. It was all too much for Richard to deal with especially with the demands of the Comic book Code on his back for the last two years.

---

10 Ironically Dr. Fredrick Wertham was dissatisfied with the code wanting a rating system instead.

Dicky would say that his father, "was really frustrated with the silly rules that the code had. It got so bad that he forgot that he even had a second son! My younger brother Jake was born two years before the accident and pretty much ended up getting forgotten as a result of the whole turbulence of the decade.

"It's hard to really gauge what was going on with all the chaos and what not. It got to the point were the only writing my dad could do was those Koltar stories. That was the only time he could have joy in his work. Then he decided to make all the horror comics into black and white comic magazines. That helped get the comic code off his back on those comics but he was creatively drained by then. The only bit of creativity at the time he could get out of his skull was within the Koltar stories."

Fighting depression and writer's block after two years of fighting the Comic Code Richard got desperate and decided to make his twelve year old son the head writer of WCI. It was a gambit that could either work or would simply destroy WCI leaving Industrial Pulps the only thing left in the Winecrest mini-Empire.[11] A lot of pressure would be on young Dicky's shoulders.

Dicky recounts that he doesn't, "know how I did it. Seriously it was crazy as hell. If Stan wasn't there to help me co-write many of the early stories I wrote I don't know what I'd do. Funny thing is that it all worked out fine. Still we were all on thin ice and it really should not have worked. I mean who puts a twelve year old as the head writer of a comic book company?"

---

11 A pretty insane gambit since pulp magazines were already starting to wane in popularity by then. Most of Industrial Pulps profits came from WCI by then.

Stan was like an older brother to the young writer. Stan knew all too well what it was like being a kid working for a comic book company. He understood the dilemma of juggling work, school and a social life. Even though there was a bit of an age difference the two became best friends. They were as close friend as their fathers were.

As the rest of the decade goes by Dicky becomes a better writer and grows into a determined man. He was a determined young man with love on his mind in the summer of 1959. That love that was on his mind was for Sally Spitz, Stan's sister. This made things awkward to say the least.

As Dicky would recount that, "it was a bit odd and uneasy. I mean I was best friends with Stan and I was secretly dating his sister around the time. I was about thirteen. It was all without him knowing. We didn't know how to explain it to him. We also were worried he would disapprove since sally was a year older than me."

While that was one head ache the two lovebirds dealt with, another was the fact that Sally had a desire to draw comics while her brother didn't want her to. Her brother had at the time completely dismissed her because she was a girl. This extended to Stan refusing to ever see Sally's drawings because as a girl she couldn't draw anything good.

Sally in later years would say, "My brother back then was a chauvinist jerk. He got better but back then he was definitely a total chauvinist jerk. Ironically he now thinks I'm a better illustrator than him but back then he wouldn't even look at my work.

"Then again it was a bunch of bullshit that came out of it being the fifties. Thing is for a while I honestly started to doubt myself. I then got over it but then I thought I was the only one who thought my drawings were good. Then Dicky saw a couple of my drawings. He thought they were on the same level as my brother. At that time I thought I was

25

the only one who thought my drawings were good. Dicky proved me wrong which led me to never give up."

Dicky would also hatch a plan to send samples of Sally's work to Stan under a man's name. The idea of using a pseudonym came to Dicky because he himself used many while writing comics for WCI so as to give an impression of more than one writer working at WCI. Anyway the idea of sending the drawings under a man's name worked. Stan looked at them and liked them.

It had worked. The whole plan had worked. Stan looked at a couple of samples mailed to him under the name Jerry Johnson. Sally would draw many comics for WCI under the name Jerry Johnson for about a year. After that full year Stan would discover the ruse. In the end he would just go and shrug it off and would entirely change his mind when it came to female artists.

Close the end of the decade Dicky decided to pitch a new black and white magazine to be published by WCI. It would be a humor magazine called Convulsion[12] and it would be first published in the summer of 1959. Convulsion would feature absurdist and Surrealist styled humor.

Even Richard was interested in writing for the publication (which partially led to the thing getting green lit). Richard would come up with a feature for the comic magazine called Kitzy and Farmer. His intent was to combine what many considered high brow and low brow with a little bit of the bizarre.

The Best way to describe Kitzy and Farmer was if you took Samuel Becket's Waiting for Godot, had it set in a Salvador Dali style desert and had talking anthropomorphic cats (that resembled what can be

---

12 The famous tagline for the comic was "A comic's magazine that will give you a Convulsion."

best describe as the inbred children of Krazy Kat) replacing all human characters involved. Obviously it was another odd creation of Richard Winecrest. It proved that Richard could come up with something new after all.

Besides Kitzy and Farmer there were many other reoccurring characters and serialized strips in Convulsion. This included Waggie the living cartoon Wagon Wheel[13] whose enemy was an obvious parody of the Michelin man. There was also Sparky the broken light bulb that would accidently shock people. And that was only a small portion of characters appearing in Convulsion.

---

13 It is exactly what it sounds like.

These are some Very early and very grotesque designs of Kitzy and farmer. Possibly done by Richard Winecrest but there is no definitive proof.

Through the turbulent decade WCI had almost died, was resurrected, almost died and got resurrected again. Like a phoenix. The torch had been given to Dicky by his father Richard. A new chapter in the history of WCI was ending while another was being written.

And through it all Weird Comics Inc. had risen from the ashes it had come back in the form of a phoenix. It rose like a phoenix and expanded itself into a new and extraordinary way.

People thought that after the young son of Richard Winecrest was made head of the writing for WCI it would die off. Those cynics were completely wrong. They thought the comic code would kill WCI. Those cynics were completely wrong. They were just completely wrong.

Dicky look back says the he is, "proud of what we achieved back then. Still there was so many problems that we had to overcome I have no idea how we did it. Looking back now I'm completely surprised that we just happened to survive.

"I was so young and naïve and yet that somehow became an asset. I was able to make decisions that other people in my position would not have done. In a . . . excuse me for saying this but in a very weird way it was so helpful that I really did not understand what I was doing."

Dicky further would reflect by saying, "In a way had Wertham not happened my father wouldn't have put me in the position as head writer of WCI. So I'm surprisingly thankful for what Wertham did but I also hate him for what he did because Wertham seriously didn't know what he was talking about.

"It really pisses me off because in some ways the whole Wertham thing was worse on my dad then the accident. Wertham in some ways was worse than the accident that killed my father's dad and my father's best friend.

"I was pretty shocked to later learn that he had once argued that Albert Fish[14] shouldn't have gotten the death penalty. It really made me feel weird.

"Let me tell you that I'm a very liberal hippy kind of guy who is totally against the death penalty but if someone deserved the death penalty it was Albert Fish.

"You really need to think about how fucked up it is that a guy like Wertham who claimed to care for children by crusading against comics while previously saying a man who molested, killed and ate children shouldn't have gotten the death penalty. I'm sorry but that is pure madness. I'm honestly surprised that no one brought this shit up when Wertham was doing his whole thing back in the fifties.

"Still I will give Wertham two things. First off he was for desegregation very early on. Before most people were for it. I commend him for that. Secondly Wertham tried to make amends with the comic book fan community when he found interest in comic fanzines and that he said that he overacted.

"Still I'm not sorry for punching him in the face when I met him at a comic book convention in 1972. One bad thing that came out of the fifties was the fact that my dad kind of went crazy with grief over everything. That led to him ignoring my brother which was a real shame. For a while he didn't even know he existed.

"I was the golden boy who was following in my father footsteps at an early age while my brother was the forgotten one. I was always trying my best to make it up to my brother as a sort of surrogate father. I know that all I've said is a bit random but that's what I think of when I think of the 1950's. It's a bunch of random stuff."

---

14 A serial killer who would molest, kill and then eat children.

Chapter 4

Superheroes come back in style at WCI

The sixties would bring a large change in comics along with the change in culture at large. Superheroes would come back in style. Sally and Dicky who both had always loved the early superhero comic book work of their respective fathers had always wanted to make some superhero comics.

They devised to do just that with a new comic to be published in 1964 called All New American Heroes. This title would have three features in it featuring three very different superheroes that would occupy the comic.

First off was a revival of the obscure Golden Age character Moonchild. It was co-written by Dicky and Sally while Sally illustrated it. Moonchild would be presented as the same character as she was when she was in the forties.

She was revealed to have been the survivor of a plot in which The LSP were established to be stuck in a Limbo like state since the late forties. She was the only one who had escaped but was not able to free her fellow teammates from their fate. She was a girl of the forties living in the sixties.

Moonchild was also given a new sidekick called Tiger Moon who was of course a tiger who also happened to talk. Moonchild was also given new powers that made her have control over the domain of dreams. Though she didn't understand her purpose and powers at first she quickly was able to defend the dream world. For she was intended to take care of the dream world while evil nightmares would try and take over the dream world.

A more disgusting character in the book was Slimbo a character that was a blob of goo that fought crime. Originally intended to be a living pile of snot it was changed to generic goo after the comic book code made some noise over the character. It was a feature that many saw as the weakest link in the comic. It had been created by Dicky's younger brother Jake when Jake was twelve.

As time went on Slimbo would slowly turn into a character worthy of being printed by WCI but his early stories were definitely juvenile. It didn't help that Jake had to work in the shadow of his older brother Dicky. It made it harder since Dicky had written better comics at the same age. Cruel comparisons overtook any legitimate criticism.

Dicky recounts that, "I originally put Jake on as a writer because I felt bad for him. Our dad loved me and had put me into a position of power at WCI. It didn't help that I was a successful writer. Jake felt left out.

"On top of that my dad would frequently forget Jake existed. Anyway some might say that the early Slimbo stories were trash but I'd say they were much better than people gave them credit for.

"Sure in the beginning I was really trying to make up for stuff for my brother. I even based the Crimson Protector on Jake and gave the Crimson Protector Jake's birthday. I want people to remember that Jake became a great writer as time went on."

The third feature/character found in All New American Heroes was the previously mention Crimson Protector. To fully give a well rounded explanation of the character at large would amount to a lot of space dedication into needing to explain the Crimson Protector's origin and his history (at the very least his history in the decade of the 60's would take a lot of time to explain).

The character was intended to have a mysterious origin. All that was set up was that his mother was an alien from a solar system that had been destroyed. Beyond that it was intended to be a complete mystery to the audience. This meant there would be no full origin for the character until 1970 when All New American Heroes was retiled The Crimson Protector & The Galactians.

Pregnant at the time of the destruction of her solar system The Crimson Protector's Mother would go to earth. She would go there intending to live as a human. Pregnant at the time of the destruction she would to earth and live as a human. She would give birth to her son and name him Ted Thompson. Like Jake the character of Ted Thompson was born on June 13th 1952.

As the origin goes shortly after Ted's birth his widowed alien mother meets and later marries an escapist named Tommy Tedson. By the age of ten Ted was able to do amazing stunts on his own that amaze his step-father. These stunts are because of his superpowers. Ted soon started doing escape stunts with his step-father. Ted's mother keeps him in the dark when it comes to her past and why Ted has superpowers.

Soon in 1962 Ted's younger half sister Molly (who displays no superpowers) is born. While at the time she would not have a major role in the comics she would grow up to become the super heroine known as Energy Woman.

Anyway more time goes on and by the time Ted is twelve his powers are fully manifested. These powers include super strength, the ability to fly, the ability to melt things with his mind, be able to have enhanced ventriloquism, and an ability to escape any trap no matter how tricky.

With his newfound abilities Ted wonders what to do with his newfound abilities until one day when he finds an old tattered comic. The comic features Koltar the Mighty Immortal. Ted reads the comic and decides to become a superhero. He then takes an old escape artist costume designed by his mother and converts it into a superhero costume.

With that Ted starts to clean up the town he lives in (a bizarre version of Chicago, Illinois that was a combination of art deco with elements of what would later be called a steam punk and diesel punk[15]) and he goes by the name the Crimson Protector.

While the Crimson Protector is an archetypical superhero there are several things that make him interesting especially when considering the personal aspect of his creation. For instance the fact that the hero was meant to be somewhat modeled on Jake Winecrest as a sort of gift to Jake was unique in the Crimson Protector creation.

Then of course over time the character of the Crimson Protector became more and more like Dicky Winecrest. Another personal aspect was the fact that the Crimson Protector was inspired by Koltar the Mighty Immortal (a character Richard Winecrest had always said was his favorite creation).

As Dicky would put it, "I was very conscious in having Ted become the Crimson Protector by being inspired by a comic of Koltar the Mighty Immortal. Koltar's own origin had him finding a comic and deciding to become a superhero.

"I wanted that personal connection between the characters. In a weird way I thought that by making the Crimson Protector that way. Y'know by making the character both inspired by Koltar and making him like my brother might make a difference.

---

15 Steam Punk and Diesel Punk are two distinct science fiction sub-genres that would be coined many years after the initial debut of The Crimson Protector. The version of Chicago in the Crimson Protector stories can only be (in my opinion) best compared to the visual worlds presented in those two sub-genres of science fiction along with an art deco esthetic.

"I felt that it might make a difference between my Brother and Father. Y'know like it might have been able to have my brother and my father get a little bit closer. Obviously that didn't happen. I obviously was wrong in thinking that way. I was really naïve at the time."

As Dicky failed to help create a connection between his father and brother, the Crimson Protector was a success. Letters came in revealing his overall popularity. Readers liked the wide range of stories that the Crimson Protector was in.

The stories that featured the Crimson Protector ranged from stories about Ted balancing his personal life with his life as a superhero to gimmicky type of stories. Such gimmicks would vary to such things as the mischievous wizard Yodell Mai Godell turning ted into various creatures, various historical figures up because of the inventions of evil junior scientist Dex Dezmond, robots from space eating gold, storm clouds that rained television sets, Ted having to cross-dress to infiltrate mobsters with advanced technology and drinking water turning the population of Chicago purple for a short amount of time. On top of all this Ted had to deal with being a teenager in the sixties. The stories that Ted were featured in were extremely odd even by the standards of most comic books created within the decade of the sixties.

As time went on the supporting characters to the Crimson Protector was introduced. In 1967 the Crimson Protector was given an animal sidekick called the Crimson Penguin. The Crimson Penguin also known as Peng had gained powers similar to the Crimson Protector through a freak accident caused by Dex Dezmond.

In 1968 Peng was given his own short-lived feature in All New American Heroes. In 1968 another younger half sister was introduce named April. April would have superpowers and would get her own short-lived feature in All New American Heroes in 1969 as Crimson Tot. Later she would grow up to become Crimson Lass.

With lots of success from the Crimson Protector Dicky and Sally decided to settle down in 1966. They bought a home with the money that the new comics brought in. Sure they wouldn't officially tie the knot for years but they were in love all the same.

Sally has said that, "it was pretty much Dicky's whole idea that we buck tradition and not get married right away. He was kind of turning into a hippy.

"I respected his wishes at the time. I understood that Dicky felt that if we got married that I'd be shackling myself to the marriage. It was an understandable opinion at the time. I would agree that it would be true if I had married some chauvinist Neanderthal. The thing is that Dicky wasn't like that but I humored him at the time.

"I humored him at the time because I did and still do love him. He just didn't understand my feelings on the matter and I understood that so I didn't fault him for it. Still I knew he'd eventually understand how I really felt and not how he thought I felt.

"The problem was that he was second guessing how I felt about getting married. He sometimes has trouble picking up on other people's feelings. He eventually apologized for the whole misunderstanding.

"When you get down to it Dicky had a very fragile psyche. He needed to be coddled and humored. That's just the way he was. He's gotten so much better over the years. It just took him a while to just mellow out and not feel like he had to assume what was best for everyone.

"He would even assume what was best for his brother and his father. I wasn't the only one Dicky would try to figure out what was best for them. It wasn't that he was controlling it was just that he cared about the people he loved so much that he'd assume what was best for all of us."

When I asked about all this she just happened to pause. She thought a real long while and then didn't say anything. At least that's what I believe at first until I notice that she seems to be trying to say something but stops before she says anything. She stops this and becomes silent.

A long lived silence fills the room. Then I ask her again if she thinks Dicky will not like me putting this into the book she replies, "I am 100% sure that he won't be bothered by me talking about it since he himself has commented on it from time to time. It's not like this is the sort of thing that might embarrass him. I'm pretty sure it won't embarrass him or my son. I'm pretty sure of that."

I honestly don't know how to react to that. I decide to go on. It was a very uncomfortable interview. The next day I asked her about it and she claim it took her a long time to think about it because she had swallowed a fly. She added that she felt the whole line of questioning was silly. I tended to agreed and decided to go onto the next aspect of the history of Weird Comics Incorporated and I will. Just forget this little speed bump and just read the next paragraph. Just read the next paragraph and learn about WCI.

Anyway in the meantime the success of All New American heroes led to WCI making a huge decision in one of their titles. They would reshape the long floundering Science to Amaze into The Science Adventures of Jason Jonze on Mars. The overly long title was of course the idea of Richard Winecrest who had fully conceived the idea of the comic and wrote it.

The Amazing Science Adventures of Jason Jonze on Mars was Richard Winecrest's first new creation since the since discontinued Convulsion Magazine feature Kitzy and Farmer. At the time Richard only wrote Koltar stories (which had recently been moved to All New American Heroes). Richard wanted to really stretch himself as a creative force. The Jason Jonze comic stared a black scientist who builds his own rocket ship to mars and helps the native Martians be freed from slavery imposed by the hostile dictator King Rutpo.

Sure there was some elements taken form Edgar Rice Burrough's Mars tales but there were two aspects that were unique for the time. A black lead in a comic set on mars was unheard of in the sixties. The other unique aspect was the amount of issues to tell a story.

Richard wrote the series in a slow pace in a way that decades later would be termed decompression.[16] This kind of storytelling would not be attempted within American comics for a couple of Decades. Obviously the two aspects that made the comic unique had also most likely doomed the comic to only be six issues.

Dicky Winecrest recalls that, "It devastated my dad that it didn't last. He loved the series so much. He loved it so much that he published the rest of the issues that mad up the first story arc even though it was losing money. He felt helpless since by this time the pulp publishing side of things was quickly dying off.

All that was left was WCI. With that all he had to do was write Koltar stories. It just all happened at around the same time and that

---

16 Decompression is a style of storytelling found in comics which typically has slower pacing and will have storylines take place over many issues. This form of storytelling came to prominence in comics during the 1990's.

affected my dad. Besides that I have no idea how to really explain what happened to him."

There would be several comics in the eighties that continued the adventures of Jason Jonze written by Dicky but Richard would only write Koltar related comic stories from then on. For the rest of Richard's life he would only write stories staring Koltar the Mighty Immortal. Richard would not try and create any new creations. For better or for worse Koltar would be all that Richard had left.

In February of 1968 things at WCI were really shaken up when Dicky would meet Alejandro Vasquez. Vasquez was an underground cartoonist from San Francisco who Dicky had met. Vasquez would claim to anyone who would listen to him that he had met the likes of Jerry Garcia and Hunter S. Thompson (though to what extent is debatable). He was a big shot in the underground comix world and he was oddly enough interested in working at WCI.

The meeting between the two would not only result in Dicky hiring Vasquez but Dicky also making an odd change on one of WCI's comics. Convulsion magazine had always been an oddity among the comics published by WCI but with Dicky meeting Vasquez he felt it should go into a more odd direction. He wanted it to be more like some of the underground comix Vasquez made.

So Dicky wanted to turn Convulsion into the first (and possibly only) color underground comix magazine published by a (somewhat) major comic book company (despite all that being an oxymoron).

The magazine which had been in black and white up until that point had ended up being on its last legs. The comic really happened to be in a sever need of a jolt in the pants. It had also been widely criticized at the time for its lack of surrealism and absurdism within its pages in the last few years of its publication prior to the time in which Alejandro Vasquez was brought onboard.

Dicky felt the change would be the trick. The magazine had always had surreal cartoons but with Vasquez co-editing the magazine it became decidedly more adult. The distribution quickly changed from being on newspaper racks to being in head shops as a result of the change in content.

Most of what permeated in this new era of Convulsion was largely comedic though there was an exception in Freak Squad. It featured four very odd superheroes. It featured characters such as Tom Hologram (who didn't have anything to do with holograms, that was just his name), Snotty the Snot Man, Nukey the Nuke Boy and Annie A (a woman who could control her armpit hair that was as strong as steel).

Vasquez has recently recalled that, "most people working in underground comics at the time had a lukewarm to hatred kind of attitude towards superheroes.[17] I was one of the few exceptions. I was an even a further exception in that I was the only one who wanted to do a non-parody superhero comic.[18] Anyway I approached Dicky with the idea of doing a superhero team comic for Convulsion. He really dug my approach. He thought it made too much sense.

"I wanted to do it outside of the comic book code so Convulsion seemed the place to put it in especially since I was co-editing it with Dicky at the time. He agreed since he wanted to write superhero comics in a way that he couldn't with the code in place. We really wanted to see what kind of weird stuff we could do with superheroes and the Code would just get in the way, man.

---

17 I will admit this is debatable. Still this is Mr. Vasquez's opinion.
18 Again this is merely Mr. Vasquez's opinion.

"So I said let's do a superhero team inspired by freak shows.[19] Dicky said he had some ideas that would fit in with that and the fact we wanted to write something outside of the comic book code.

"First off he suggested Snotty the Snot Man which was based on an earlier idea for Slimbo in which Slimbo was made of snot which had been axed by the code. They said it was too disgusting for print so that became the first suggestion Dicky made to me.

"Then Dicky suggested Annie A who was a really odd character. She was a chick who had this like living armpit hair that was as strong as steel. Sometimes I was afraid of some of Dicky's ideas.

"Nukey the Nuke Boy was my idea. He was a kid who was so irradiated that he had to wear a special suite so he wouldn't kill anyone. He was intended to be a tragic character since he couldn't have physical contact with anyone or he'd accidently happen to kill them. He also could shoot radiation in a controlled beam that had some dots in the beam like those Kirby dots or whatever. It was cool to draw him.

"Anyway when Dicky first mentioned Tom Hologram and described him as a hallucinogen taking former journalist who happened to be a superhero I just thought Hunter S. Thompson. Though it did seem to not conform to the whole freak show concept I thought he would make an interesting character anyway. I used to hang out with Thompson so that's why the character is the way he is."

Dicky recalls that he, "decided on Tom being inspired by Hunter S. Thompson long before I pitched the thing to Alejandro. I just made him think it was his idea since he always claimed to have met Thompson back

---

19 Dicky contends that he suggested a freak show theme for the team after Vasquez approached him wanting to do a superhero comic in Convulsion.

in his days living in San Francisco. Thing is Vasquez usually remembers things differently then how they happened. I'd blame the psychedelic drugs but that would give his imagination too little credit."

A feature solely contributed by Dicky was a one page comic called Crazy Jack that Dicky both wrote and drew. It was a very odd comic about a crazy janitor. He was an odd protagonist considering some of the violent and ugly things he would do. Anyway I will talk more about it in the next chapter in which I detail aspects of the Crazy Jack movie created in the seventies.

Anyway another feature that Vasquez contributed to the new version of Convulsion was the Heroin Brothers, a darkly humorous feature that stared two heroin addicts.

It was controversial even among the new fans of the book. Some felt it was too preachy against drugs while some felt it glorified hard drugs. In many ways this very feature was what possibly doomed the new version of Convulsion.

A drawing of Crazy Jack that Dicky made for me.

This new version of Convulsion ended spectacularly with a Freak Squad story in which everyone on the team except for Tom Hologram got killed off in an atomic blast. Tom survived though confined to a wheelchair because he had already survived an atomic blast as part of his origin (in which he rode an atomic bomb while tripping on psychedelic drugs). This did not explain why Nukey the Nuke Boy happened to die in the blast.

In an odd way this seemed to serve as an interesting end to an intriguing decade for WCI.

Chapter 5

Always Expanding and Always Reshuffling, Always

n the seventies WCI wanted to yet again reshuffle things around. Dicky felt it was important to make some changes to herald in the new decade. First off he wanted to introduce a new reprinting program. These reprints would be known as the WCI Vault Collections.

Most people would not remember the name but that wasn't the point. The point was to release earlier comics in a big book. The first comic series/character to be collected by the WCI Vault Collections were a lot of the early Koltar stories. This was something that most people predicted when it was announced that there would be a line of book recollecting earlier comics published by WCI.

Dicky decided that besides starting the WCI Vault Collections that he would need to publish some new comics under WCI. So WCI would need to launch some new titles to ring in the new decade. Dicky had decided that the first new title to be launched by WCI was to be a revival of The Legion Society of Protectors (now simply published as The LSP).

In a 1968 comic The LSP had been freed by Moonchild. This had been within a story staring Moonchild. And even though the LSP had been introduced in that Moonchild story they didn't get their own comic for a long time. They would appear off and on in stories featuring Moonchild until they were given their own comic in 1970.

In the new comic staring The LSP many changes would happen. In the debut issue of the revival of The LSP Starry Knight would get married to Mary Crawford. Mary Crawford was a woman that Starry Knight met and had been dating since shortly after The LSP escaped Limbo in 1969. The two characters would have a son. Frank would be born a year later and would later become an important part of the main WCI universe.

Another change was the departure of The Gray Apparition from the team known as The LSP. After which he changed his name to simply The Apparition. This ended up happening because he had become a disenfranchised loner/vigilante.

After that the character would soon be moved to the black and white noir style comic magazine Noir Boiled. This happened to be somewhat something of a controversy at the time. When you get down to it the whole thing would be somewhat that was not something that many would not forget.

In the meantime Dicky was introducing new things into the pages of The LSP. After decades of uncertainty of Moonchild's origin she was finally given an origin. It was revealed that she was a descendant of a race of cosmic beings created by a near omnipotent race to protect the dreams of humans. This was considered pretty heady stuff for mainstream superhero comics (even by the standards of the seventies).

Starry Knight was also given a proper origin (besides him just merely having the sword Excalibur). He was revealed to have been a descendant of King Arthur. It was also revealed that the descendants of Arthur were cursed to do good to make up for the fall of Camelot as a result of Arthur's indiscretions. This would lead to the launching of the black and white Sword and Sorcery comic magazine The Brazen Sword of Arthur.

The comic magazine The Brazen Sword of Arthur would feature stories in both a sword and sorcery vein and those in a weird fiction vein. These stories would stare Arthur Pendragon in various points of his life. Backups for The Brazen Sword of Arthur included black and white reprints of stories from WCI's fifties era monster comics magazine Science Monster as well as other types of stories. These other stories would include features featuring other stories that featured many generic sword and sorcery characters as well.

There was a critique at the time (and since) that some of the more generic comic stories published in The Brazen Sword of Arthur proved that many of the creators working on the title didn't care about what was being published at the time besides the (fantastic) Arthur stories. There were many odd stories published within the pages of The Brazen Sword of Arthur that many felt wouldn't have been published anywhere or any other time in WCI's history.

An example of one of these generic stories feature a generic sword and sorcery character finding a tied up woman who was about to be eaten by a large turtle with a fruit tree (though it look more like a palm tree with fruit on it growing out of the turtles shell). The man slays the giant turtle and then eats the fruit.

Then the man is paralyzed and then eaten by the woman he just saved. It is revealed that she was a demon tricking the hero into "saving" her and to eat the turtle's fruit. It was intended to be an ironic ending but many thought it was just stupid. That story left many feeling like Dicky wasn't even trying.

Dicky asserts now that he could, "agree that some of the more generic stories not featuring Arthur weren't my best but I liked the one with the Giant turtle.[20] I really was trying my hardest. Still everything else I wrote at the time at WCI was pretty solid. Just look at any issue from The LSP or The Crimson Protector & the Galactians from the same period or any other I wrote back then."

The Crimson Protector & the Galactians was what All New American Heroes was renamed after The Crimson Protector was the

---

20 If you ask me (no intention to offend Dicky but) that story is probably the weakest thing Dicky's written.

only hero form the comics launch left.[21] With this change also came some major changes and revelations for Ted/Crimson Protector.

First off his mother finally told him his origin. Not only was both of his parent aliens but they were both alien royalty. Ted's birthfather was the King of Crimson (of the planet Crimson) and his mother was (the original) Energy Woman.[22] It was also revealed that they were part of a group of heroes formed by the royalty of several planets within the Sye System, solar system many light years away from earth.

This group was presented (in the stories) as originally being called The Princes of the Universe until the inclusion of female members (the original) Energy Woman, (the original) Futura of the planet Futurist and Gravitia of the planet Tia. It was then decided that the team would be rechristened The Galactians which also featured members such as The Purple Piper of the planet Purple, and the feuding brother Aqualung and The Holy Diver of the planet Oceanica.

The Galactians served as protector's of the Sye System. Then one day the Sye System would be under attack from a threat they couldn't stop. A biomechanical creator only known as Cylord appeared. Cylord fed off the power of stars. He particularly chose stars big enough to serve as suns for solar systems. When he sucked out the energy of these stars he would emit a blast that would destroy solar systems.

Most inhabitants of planets in the Sye System fled to other planets before Sye's destruction but The King of Crimson stayed hoping to find a way to save the Sye System. Shortly thereafter he is betrayed by the Purple Piper because Cylord promises the Purple Piper powers beyond his belief. Cylord of course lied and proceeded to kill the Purple Piper

---

21 Slimbo by this time had been moved to Noir Boiled while Moonchild was now only relegated to being a member of The LSP.

22 Ted's half-sister Molly would become the second Energy Woman.

along with the King of Crimson in a giant explosion destroying all of the Sye System.

Dicky has admitted that much of the ideas for the Galactian's and the Crimson Protector's backgrounds came to him in an almost random trance. He would claim that he got the ideas meditating. Sally questions this many times claiming that Dicky would pace around in his underwear and exclaim ideas that would later for into stories form The Crimson Protector and the Galactians.

Sally would claim that many an idea would come from Dicky because of his odd way of doing things. Dicky has always stated that this was never so. Still Dicky has done a lot of odd things in his life. For instance how Cylord was thought up is up to much debate though according to Sally it's an interesting story. Sally's version of events led one to believe that Dicky was in line for the groceries one day and he noticed something. He noticed a cheese grader. Looking at the cheese grader he wondered if he could make it into a character. He wondered if he could make it into a living being. Dicky claims this is false and that he always had invented Cylord early Crimson Protector days but this is debatable.

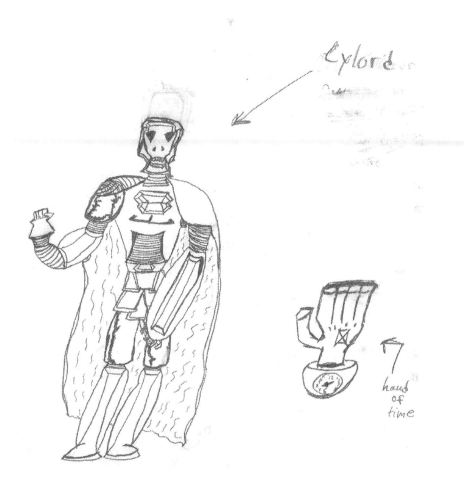

Cylord

hand
of
time

A design for Cylord that Dicky gave to Stan Spitz as a reference of what Dicky wanted. Also features a design for the Hand of Time a device intended originally to feature in a later storyline that never came to be.

This revelation about Ted led to the next two changes to the comic. Ted as the Crimson Protector would then decide to change his costume to look more like his birth father's royal garb.[23] Ted also grows a moustache to more resemble his birth father.[24] Ted would hide his moustache in his civilian life thanks to a device created by Professor Perfect a large headed scientist that would later work for The LSP.

The last change made to the title was the introduction of a new team of Galactians form by the children of the original group. The Crimson Protector would join their ranks. This would lead to stories featuring them all.

These stories would serve as a backup feature to the main Crimson Protector stories. The roster of members of the new version of the Galactians were Grav (son of Gravitia), Aquena (daughter of the Holy Diver), and a new Futura (daughter of the first and who in her earth civilian identity as a struggling model in which she went by the name Ana).

The status queue lasted through the whole decade until The Galactians were given their own comic when The Crimson Protector and Ana/Futura left the group (in turn changing the title of The Crimson Protector & The Galactians to The Crimson Protector & Futura).

---

23 It is also revealed that Ted's mother designed his escapist costume to already look like the royal garb that the King of Crimson wore. Still Ted wants his costume to look even more like his father's royal garb.

24 By this time Jake Winecrest had grown a moustache and Dicky wanted The Crimson Protector to reflect this.

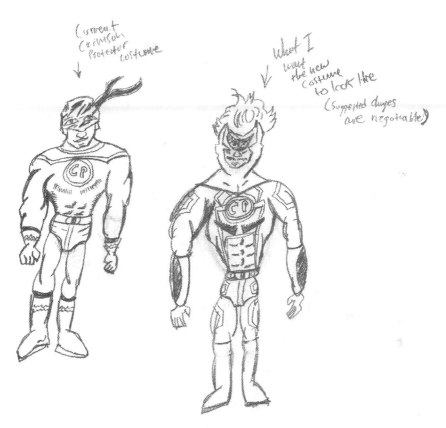

A drawing done by Dicky Winecrest to show a comparison with the then current Crimson Protector design and what he wanted Stan to put into the new redesign. Note the new moustache!

The departure of the two was a result of the two marrying in 1978 and the two deciding to only focus on villains on earth. This was a controversial decision to say the least. Mostly it was the decision to have the two focus solely on earth when it came to their crime fighting.

Though some still argue about having the two marry (but that was a small minority compared to those who were ticked that The Crimson Protector and Futura would not have any more cosmic adventures[25]). All in the entire buzz generated buzz for WCI anyway.

Shortly thereafter Ted's half-sister Molly who up until that point in the comic's history seemed to have no superpowers had discovered she had latent powers that had just recently appeared. She then decided to wear an altered version of her mother's Energy Woman costume[26] and become the new Energy Woman.

While beautiful she was brash, tough as nails and didn't take guff from no one. She would quickly be given her own comic which would last from 1978-1983. She was also given a spot in The LSP after she turned down an offer to join the Galactians.

---

25 This would settle down since the two would later have several adventures in space again. Also after a while after Dicky had a hard time writing a husband and wife superhero team Dicky decided to split the comic in two with half the comic being dedicated to The Crimson Protector and the other Half to Futura. The title would be later simply The Crimson Protector when Futura would get her own title shortly after the birth of Futura and the Crimson Protector's son in 1980.

26 The only difference being a big diamond shaped hole that showed off her cleavage. It was a controversial addition added by Stan Spitz who had illustrated Molly's first appearance as Energy Woman.

This is an extremely rough design of Energy Woman 2.
Stan Spitz claims to have been drunk when he illustrated
it accounting for its shoddy quality. Also notice how badly
preserved it is.

Dicky's next decision after the work on launching new titles and reinventing old ones came with an odd decision. Dicky decided to revive Freak Squad as a comic book code approved comic book. All Dicky did was ignore Tom Hologram's previous history with psychedelic drugs. Surprisingly this omission was all that was needed to secure this new version of Freak Squad being able to receive a comic book code approved seal of approval.

In this new version of the team Tom was made de facto leader (while Annie A was the leader in the previous incarnation) and was joined by a completely new set of heroes. These heroes would be very different from the group Tom had first teamed up with. They of course wouldn't be dead like the team Tom had been with. There would be even more differences than that.

First off there was a near immortal alien with extreme intelligence who looked like a kid. This kid's name was Anthony Edwards the Fourth who would constantly fool many into thinking he was a kid scientist. Anthony was accompanied by a monster bodyguard named Luthar. The team was round out by Sonny the Elastic Boy (who powers were just as one would expect) and Marrel the Mermaid (a mermaid with the power to have her tail turn into legs while on land).

While the previous version of Freak Squad was based around superheroes inspired by freak shows (except for Tom who was obviously inspired by Hunter S. Thompson) the new team intended to be a team of losers. They were the superhero team that would be approached when no other hero would help. This new version would be different in its approach to being heroes. They would even get booked for birthdays, wedding anniversaries, bar mitzvahs and bat mitzvahs. It was an odd comic to say the least (though arguably not nearly as odd as the previous incarnation of Freak Squad).

Another shake up at WCI was the launching of the black and white noir style comics magazine called Noir Boiled. It featured four serialized stories a month. Three of the four features were written by Jake Winecrest. Those stories actually fit the noir tone of the magazine while Dicky would write a comic that seemed completely different and seemed to be inserted in the magazine because there were else to publish those stories.

That odd feature starred a character named Professor Phantomos who lived in Locust, Pennsylvania. The Professor (as he was simply called in the comic) was revealed to be a forgotten magic based superhero from the 40's who had been taught magic by Merlin the wizard from Camelot.

The Professor was a semi-recovering heroin addict magician who lived with his male to female transsexual Girlfriend/Magician's Assistant Sister Ray (who would dress up like a nun during their magic act). The stories would go back and forth between the messed up personal life of the Professor (that had been inspired by the work of William S. Burroughs and the music of The Velvet Underground) and battles with cosmic demons (such as the Cosmic Bastard).

The other features in Noir Boiled written by Jake Winecrest fit more in line the name of the magazine but would still have an odd twist. Jake wrote stories staring The Apparition (the former LSP member who had turned into a disillusioned street fighting vigilante), Ron Roe (a monkey who had been sent into space and through the effects of gamma radiation have been turned into a blue colored super-intelligent ape who became a private investigator) and Slimbo (who by this time had become a body guard for hire). This was not your daddy's type of hard boiled noir stories. They were something completely different.

There has been some controversy over reprints of some of the stories from Noir Boiled. Later reprints have added some color to the comics. In these reprints color has been added to Ron Roe's (blue) skin, The Apparition's blue tie, Slimbo's (green) body, blood and other objects. Some feel this degrades the memory of the previous versions of the comic.

Dicky has always claimed that he reprints were done this way to conform to what Jake had always wanted. There are copies of Jake's scripts that do mention the inclusion of color to selected things.[27] Still discussion on the merits either way happen to this day.

Anyway in 1974 Dicky decided to publish a new version of Convulsion again. But Dicky had learned his lesson in some ways. This time Convulsion would appear as it did prior to its color days. Crazy Jack was brought back too (though this time illustrated by someone other than Dicky). This would lead to success. So much so that animator Serge Bukowksi was interested in directing an animated film about Crazy Jack.

By this time Crazy Jack had gone from a sympatric crazy simpleton janitor who merely accidently would kill animals into a full blown homicidal maniac. It was one of Convulsion's more darkly humorous features. Bukowski would pay Dicky enough money for the rights to the character that Dicky was able to buy a house for Sally and himself.

In the year 1976 after many setbacks the Crazy Jack movie was released in theaters. It was both a commercial and critical bomb. Critics ravaged it for many reasons. It was derided for being too dark while others said that Serge Bukowski was merely a poor man's Ralph Bakshi. At the time the film was a total bomb. In later years it would

---

27 Something that at the time wouldn't have been possible for a black and white comic book magazine but Jake put into the scripts anyway.

gain a large cult following. Those at WCI didn't care because most were just glad the movie was actually completed.

In 1978 Sally and Dicky would get married. During this time Sally would decide to follow her dream of writing and illustrating children's picture books. She would work less on comics with only a minimal amount of comic book output during the rest of WCI's existence. Sally's first children's book was Go Cat Go in which a saxophone playing anthropomorphic cat plays the saxophone and teaches children about the history of Jazz.

Anyway before I finish the chapter I want to talk about one last comic that was launched in the seventies by WCI (there were many more than I've mentioned but I only have so much room to mention so many). That comic that I want to talk about is The Double Duo. The Double Duo (which debuted in 1974) was about two heroes named The Space and Dr. Mapleleaf.

The space was a robot that had the cosmic presence of a dead alien who was a golden age superhero. The robot also had the brain of Akira Sakai a thirteen year old that died of a mysterious disease. Dr. Mapleleaf was a Canadian scientist named Byrnes Johnson who found mystical armor with a maple leaf on its chest plate. They were a superhero odd couple that fought crime with their own brand of fun. It was a hit.

With the many successful series WCI published in the seventies it would move on into the eighties. I had seemed despite the failure of The Crazy Jack movie WCI would survive.

Chapter 6

The Big Ole' Eighties

hen the eighties came around Dicky felt that like the beginning of the previous decade he needed to shake things up. This time he decided he would shake up the dynamic of The Double Duo. The Double Duo had started to lose sales around the time. As a result Dicky thought to bring in Jim Von Bakerson as the new artist on the title.

Quickly thereafter Dicky decided to drop Dr. Mapleleaf and turn him into a villain while introducing a new hero who would serve as a new partner for The Space. In the story Dr. Mapleleaf ate a phoenix's egg which ended up turning him into a super villain (leading to him never becoming a hero again). To fight the new villain version of Dr. Mapleleaf The Space teamed up with a Harlem based scientist Obadiah Hughes.

Hughes was a scientist who had developed a suit that makes normal humans be able to reach extreme speeds with no adverse side effects. Hughes then dons the suite and calls himself Speedbolt. Then The Space and Speedbolt defeat Dr. Mapleleaf. Dr. Mapleleaf refuses to go by the name Dr. Mapleleaf again and would from then on only go by his real name Byrnes Johnson.

In the same year that these changes were being made a twelve page backup feature was introduced into the pages of The Double Duo.[28] The new backup stories would star the character Jason Jonze. The first stories featured in the backup take place right after the aftermath of the events at the ending of the original Jason Jonze series but quickly then take place in (what was then) Modern times. Jim Von Bakerson worked as artist on the backup as well.

---

28 Now dubbed The New Double Duo, though no changes to the issue numbering is made.

Jim von Bakerson has said that he, "really enjoyed doing the Jason Jonze stories. Sure I loved illustrating The New Double Duo but I always had a special place in my heart for the original Jason Jonze comics that Dicky's dad wrote. It was a real inspiration for me as a black kid growing up in the sixties.

"Still Dicky and I wanted to do our own take on the character. Although I love the original stories they are a bit . . . unsubtle. I mean when you get down to it the original series was about a black scientist who builds a rocket ship to get to mars to get away from the discrimination of the time and then frees a race of Martians who are enslaved. That's obviously not subtle at all. The stories Dicky and I wanted to do were meant to be more of a straight adventure strip in contrast.

"I came up with the idea that he had a fourteen year old daughter who was half Martian. There was that one scene in the original comic that we sorta hinted at was when she was conceived. But what was more important was that I wanted this idea that there would be conflict between father and daughter.

"Dicky liked that idea and decided to name her Mary. Then later on he decided to rename her Cross-Eyed Mary when she joined Freak Squad. He said he got the idea since like all Martians Mary had no iris. I still don't know how I feel about both those decisions. I was ok when she married The Space but the new name and her being in Freak Squad just felt off. Still I respect Dicky as a co-creator."

Around this time Dicky wanted to launch a new Crimson Protectors spinoff. One of the first things he had decided to do was give Futura her own title after the birth of her (and Ted's) son.[29] This would turn

---

29 Which coincided with the birth of Dicky and Sally's son Waldo Richard Winecrest V (simply known as Waldo after his grandfather).

The Crimson Protector into a solo book once again. Dicky had also decided to have Ted's youngest sister Suzy become Crimson Lass. She was quickly given her own book and joined with the Crimson Penguin as her sidekick.

Some say the Crimson Protector's own comic became stagnant at this time while others say it was the best years in the comic's history. One aspect added to the comic that has been a subject of controversy amongst fans of The Crimson Protector was him taking up smoking.

Dicky's decision to turn the Crimson Protector into a smoker accounted to two reasons. First was the fact that the comic book code was softening at the time and Dicky wanted to see what he could get away with. The other reason was that by that time Jake Winecrest had started smoking and Dicky wanted the comic to reflect it.

In 1983 WCI bought the rights to publish an English translation of the mature French Sci Fi/Fantasy comic magazine Fantastic Iron. Dicky would also bring on some of the original French artists to illustrate stories written by American creators working at WCI.

For instance Jim Von Bakerson would write a controversial comic feature titled "A God am I?" which featured an amnesiac black Jesus stuck in a dystopian cyberpunk future. Dicky would at the time write a feature called Android Revolution in which an android originally intended as a sex toy helps the last remnant of the enslaved human race. Stan Spitz also wrote the fairly conventional (for Fantastic Iron) feature called Space Cadet that followed the life of a space cadet in a none linear order.

The only previously published series to feature in this American version of Fantastic Iron was Koltar the Mighty Immortal. In these new stories were set in the far flung future (approximately a whole generation before Koltar was born). This all made sense seeing as

Koltar was an immortal. Fantastic Iron would be the last publication published by WCI featuring Koltar.

These new Koltar stories would be illustrated by the French artist Cercle de Pi (a pseudonym by the way). He and Richard would craft new stories that were different than any previous incarnation of the character. These new Koltar stories were more philosophical than anything Richard had ever written. Many would say the stories were influenced by Richard's age and him dealing with his own mortality. They were also influenced by the newly found freedom that Richard had without the code.

Shortly thereafter underground musician Tony Liable[30] had a new band called Binary Hell. They were a band that could be best described as New Wave meets Heavy Metal. Liable had ties to artist Alejandro Vasquez (from Vasquez's time living in England). As such Liable wanted to do something with WCI.

Liable wanted WCI to do a comic book insert for Binary Hell's debut album. After that he also wanted WCI to do a comic book insert for Binary Hell's second/last album.[31] Both albums failed but Dicky ended up becoming pen pals with Liable. They keep in contact to this day.

While all this was happing WCI was offered a deal with the Japanese film/television company Bonsai Entertainment. They approached WCI

---

30 An American born musician who moved to England in the 60's and then became known for being in a variety of bands with such diverse musical output as Proto-Punk, Psychedelic Punk, Prog Rock, and Heavy Metal (just to name a handful of the many genres of Rock he has explored). He is called the grandfather of Avante Garde Psychedelic Prog Punk Metal. He prefers to simply be called a Rock Musician.

31 Both would be illustrated by Stan Spitz with Dicky co-writing them with Tony Liable.

with the idea to adapt The LSP into a live action Japanese superhero Tokusatsu TV Show. The show would run from 1981 to 1984 (a slightly long show by the standards of other shows of the type on Japanese television).[32] The whole thing (along with many toys) led to WCI getting lots of money.

The whole endeavor was very successful. It would make butt loads of money. Making money that would help WCI in the long run. This money that was made off the show/toys would help WCI through many hardships that would come in their later years.

In 1984 Freak Squad ends up canceled after floundering sales. Freak Squad would not be published by WCI again until the 1990's. This ends up depressing Dicky. His reaction is to create an epic cosmic mini-series so that he could get his mind off of the canceling of Freak Squad. That mini-series would be called The Cosmic Turning Point.

The Cosmic Turning point (named so to signal a big change for the character published by WCI) was an eight issue maxi-series that Dicky had written in the aftermath of the cancelation of Freak Squad. The mini-series started with the appearance of Cylord and his attempt to suck energy out of the sun of earth's solar system. The Crimson Protector destroys Cylord but not before Cylord Kills both Crimson Lass and The Space (he also destroyed the planet Venus and a nameless Canadian city). Once Cylord is destroyed his dead body floats through space. He is then discovered by a creature known as The Actinic.

The Actinic is a creature best described as looking like a planet sized squid robot toy designed by Japanese Designers while being

---

32 The show is probably most known to western audiences for having an episode that featured martial artist superstar Sonny Chiba in the role of mischievous wizard Yodell Mai Godell (in this version presented as being lecherous, a portrayal that would later follow in the American comics).

crossed with HR Giger's worst nightmare. The Actinic resurrects Cylord from the dead and make Cylord more powerful. The Actinic dubs the revived Cylord as Cupola. With that the Actinic gives Cupola a new mission, to help him destroy the universe and remake it. The reason for this is revealed that The Actinic is from a universe long dead and that he longs for it wanting to remake the universe like the one he once lost.

Pretty much the rest of the eight issue maxi-series feature many of the heroes of that universe who join forces in an attempt to stop The Actinic and Cupola. They fail until the end of the series (obviously). Then near the end of the mini-series a creature appears from out of nowhere. This creature is only known as Silver Machine and it resurrects The Space (now with a new body that is more human looking and biomechanical) and Crimson Lass (now known as the Cosmic Angel). With their combined they completely destroy The Actinic and Cupola.

As soon as the maxi-series ends Bonsai Entertainment options the comic to be made into a Japanese animated feature length film. The movie is released in Japan in the summer of 1986 and then is dubbed in English and released the next year in the US. The film is both unsuccessful critically and commercially. The mini-series it was based on while commercially successful was also savaged by critics. Critics of both the comic and its anime adaptation derided it as clichéd.

Not deterred by the reaction to The Cosmic Turning Point Dicky decides to have another mini-series published shortly thereafter. In actuality it would be two mini-series that would be published concurrently. Both mini-series were closely connected and were horror related. The Series were called The LSP Vs. The Bloody Horror and Freak Squad Explore The Bloody Horror. Both mini-series would take place during the same timeframe but feature two different superhero teams react to a new threat. As could be deduced the two teams were The LSP and Freak Squad.

The two concurrent storylines would detail events caused by a cosmic demon taking over Chicago. Said demon known only as the Bloody Horror would split Chicago into two and creating two distinct new cities. Each of the two teams would be stuck in one of the two halves of the city as created by The Blood Horror.

The half of Chicago that The LSP were stuck feature ghouls and goblins and the like terrorizing the citizens of the city. But nothing went as far as being an all-ages book. This is in stark contrast to what Freak Squad experienced on their half of the city within the pages of their mini-series Freak Squad Explore the Bloody Horror. This other mini-series is best described as Freak Squad goes to hell. In that mini-series Freak Squad is put up against sadistic murderous creatures the like that could have sprung out of the mind of Clive Barker as opposed to the traditional ghouls and goblins The LSP fought in the other mini-series. Both were commercially unsuccessful and they were quickly forgotten.[33]

In 1988 British Sci Fi/Fantasy author Nyles Norton proposes to WCI the idea for an original Graphic Novel set outside of continuity starring Moonchild. WCI approves the project and assigns art duties to Sally Spitz-Winecrest. This becomes her first work in comics since she had started making children's picture books (it also ends up being her second to last work in comics). The results is an odd and surreal comic book that while financially unsuccessful is a critic's darling and

---

33 Although an extremely small cult following has been maintained over the years.

becomes very influential on many other comics published in the years to come.

Around the same time that both Bloody Horror mini-series are released a Tragedy comes to the Winecrest family. That year Richard Winecrest and his wife June are in a car accident. History is repeating itself for Richard who had survived the car crash that took the lives of Stan Spitz and Richard's Father Waldo. Again Richard is unscathed by the accident but this time there wasn't a death involved. June went into a coma after the accident.

In grief Richard decided to write one last Koltar story. It ended up becoming the most depressing comic Richard ever wrote. In the story a close friend of Koltar's dies in a hover-car accident which Koltar obviously survives (being immortal and all). Koltar is beside himself and knows that because he is immortal he cannot kill himself.

So he decides to prevent his own birth while killing his father when his father is a child. He does so but all that happens is that Koltar creates a new universe/time line in which he is never born. Koltar still lives and feeling guilty he decides to spend the rest of infinity inside a star.

Shortly after publication of the last Koltar story Richard dies in his sleep. Ironically June emerges out of her coma only a week after Richard's death. Depressed she decides to never leave her house again and seems to only occupy herself by writing a comic book script for an original Graphic Novel. The title of the comic is shaking in the Light. The comic is a surreal story about two brothers and their cat saving the world from aliens.

Once June is finished with the script she begs her son Dicky to get it illustrated and to be published by WCI. Dicky agrees so long as he can rewrite some of the script. June says she is fine with this so long as she supervises the rewrite. After finishing his rewrite Dicky asks Sally to illustrate it and she agree. Shaking in the Light becomes the last comic book Sally Spitz-Winecrest has drawn since.

Since the release of Shaking in the Light Sally has mostly relegated herself to her children's picture books. She also would write the best selling Worthington Murders under the name Agnes Harkness. Worthington was an English Butler who served under an American family while he solved murders. He was described by some as Mr. Belvedere meets Poirot.

The first Worthington novel was Parrots in the Park in which an acquaintance of Worthington's is found dead in the park surrounded by giant parrots. The police say they have no leads and so Worthington sets off to solve the case by himself. Parrots in the Park was release almost at the same time as Shaking in the Dark. Tragedy would strike by the fact that after the release of both Parrots in the Park and Shaking in the Light June Winecrest died in her sleep.

More bad news came to Dicky in 1989 when some of WCI's sales fell drastically. As a result Dicky is forced to cancel all titles accept for The LSP and The Crimson Protector.[34] How things got this bad in less of a year is a mystery to many. But what is known is that WCI is able to stay afloat publishing only two titles as a result of the money made from the Japanese live action TV version of The LSP. Sadly this isn't enough for Dicky to keep the creators working on the other WCI titles. Dicky even ends up having to fire his own brother, Jake.[35] WCI from then on would become a bare bones company for the rest of its existence.

---

34 By this time they are the only two titles published by WCI making any money.

35 Jake would soon self-publish a couple of comics until 1992.

Chapter 7

On its last legs and beyond

ith the cancelation of countless titles Dicky decided to focus on the Crimson Protector. Dicky felt that he could reinvigorate the title which while it was the most successful WCI title it hadn't had many changes since the Cosmic Turning Point Maxi-series. Dicky wanted to prove that the character was still relevant and decided to hire a new artist.[36] As Dicky would put it, "Stan wanted to retire and at the time people were complaining that the book was stale since The Cosmic Turning Point so I thought that bringing in a young artist would shake things up.

"Easier said than done, I had to deal with allot of egos before I found the kind of artist that I wanted on the title. I remember this one guy who I thought was literally certifiable. The guy wanted the Crimson Protector to make a deal with a demon that wasn't necessarily the devil but for all intents and purposes was.

"The deal with this demon would entail that the Crimson Protector sell his marriage to the demon. Then The Crimson Protector would be de-aged, his son would cease to exist, his step-father would be alive[37] and he'd have a new love interest named after the artist's yet to be born daughter.

"The guy seemed so out of it that I honestly thought this guy was from a mental hospital or something. I won't say who it was but nowadays he's working as a big wig at one of the big two comic companies. He then proceeded to do what he planned with another character. I think you know the one. Anyway it took me a while to finally find Barry. He had a good sense of design and was a good storyteller. Hell the guy still has both those qualities in spades.

---

36 Stan Spitz had already been thinking of retiring by this point.

37 An odd suggestion since Ted/Crimson Protector's Step-Father was still alive. Although that would later give Dicky the idea to kill him off.

"Guy was so good I let him co-plot some issues with me. I also liked the fact he never argued with me over the direction of the book even though I knew he sometimes disagreed with me. He respected that I was one of the original co-creators of the character."

Barry Thurston was born March 1st 1967 in Coral Gables, Florida. His family would then proceed to move to New York when Barry was eleven. Barry would start his career as a professional artist inking pages for the underground sci fi comic Cavalcade in 1986. Barry would then become the penciler on the comic in the next year and would work on it until 1989 when the comic ceased publication.

From the time that Cavalcade ended until his job working on The Crimson Protector Barry went from one independent comic to another before Dicky hired him. Barry was ecstatic seeing as The Crimson Protector was the comic that made him want to become an artist. He knew he had big shoes to fill replacing Stan Spitz but Barry was up for the challenge.

With a new artist in place Dicky started working on storylines that would make for many changes for the life of The Crimson Protector. In the comic over the next couple of years many changes are made to the comic. The Crimson Protector becomes a reserve member of The LSP. Ted and Ana/Futura's daughter is born and quickly after which she is kidnapped by a super villain scientist. The scientist experiments on her leading her to have her age sped up to five years old (both physically and mentally). The son of Futura and The Crimson Protector becomes a superhero named Kid Crimson. Kid Crimson usually gets in the way of his father but in the instance in which his younger sister is kidnapped Kid Crimson is the one to save her.

In 1991 another change came to the comic with the death of Ted's step-father (inspired by the comments from the unnamed artist who wanted to resurrect the then not dead step-father). This issue was heralded as a landmark issue. Only a week after its publication Dicky's brother, Jake was diagnosed with lung cancer. It was terminal and had already progressed rapidly through Jake's body. Jake died on Christmas Eve 1991.

Before Jake's death Jake would write a story called Golden Years. In it a superhero dying of cancer looks back on his life. It ends with the hero pressing a button attached to his chest that blows him up in an atomic blast.

Jake tried to convince Dicky to publish the story but Dicky pointed out that a man with a button on his chest that could blow himself up in an atomic blast wouldn't become a superhero. Jake respected the criticism but as a result had decided not write anything after that. Dicky has said that even though he thought there were major flaws in the story he felt guilty for not publishing it before Jake's death.

Dicky would say that, "even though it was a very flawed story I should have published it as a gift to Jake. He was dying and I should have respected his last wish."

Some have said that Dicky made the right decision in not publishing Golden Years. Would Dicky have felt the same if Jake had survived his cancer? That wasn't important what is that Dicky was beside himself when Jake died.

Looking back Dicky has said that he was, "beyond distraught. I mean my parents had just passed away a couple of years earlier. I think that I was in a very specific frame of mind that led me to want to kill of the Crimson Protector. I really felt that with Jake's death that I couldn't write the character anymore."

Dicky would decide to kill off The Crimson Protector in an original Graphic Novel that would be published in July of 1992. While somewhat inspired by Golden Years it would be its own story. Dicky still felt he needed to give Jake a posthumous co-writing credit. While he knew that a lot of art could be completed by Barry Thurston. Dicky knew that Barry couldn't draw enough pages to get the comic out by the intended July due date.

Dicky decided to bring in additional artists on the book. Depending on what kind of scene dictated which artist he would bring onboard. For instance flashbacks were done by Stan Spitz who Dicky was able to convince to get out of retirement for just this one project. The other artists besides Barry and Stan were many artists whom Dicky had previously had to let go when there was the mass amount of cancelations in 1989. Barry was wary of both the proposition of working on a story that featured the death of his favorite comic book character and the fact he would share art duties with other artists.

The comic starts with the stopping of a super villain which leads into The Crimson Protector receiving test results from Professor Perfect. These test results find that the Crimson Protector has lung cancer. Quickly thereafter The Crimson Protector tries to shrug this off as he teams up with Professor Phantomos and members of The LSP to track down The Galactic Bastard. After The Bastard is sent back to his own dimension his daughter Blood Betty sneaks through undetected.

Blood Betty proceeds to seduced, have sex with and kill men in Chicago. During this time The Crimson Protector reminisces about the past while dealing with the fact he is dying. The Crimson Protector also deals with his son's onset of puberty that leads to many awkward scenes. All this happens while The Crimson Protector tries to also help The LSP and a new version of The Freak Squad to find the mysterious killer (who is Blood Betty). While this is happening Blood Betty kills several men (including a member of the new version of Freak Squad) and none of the heroes know who the perpetrator is. It's not found out until she seduces, has sex with and attempts to kill Kid Crimson.[38] After this revelation the heroes try to stop her.

The Graphic Novel ends with The Crimson Protector defeating Blood Betty by speeding up the spread of his cancer cells so he can extract them from his body and use them as a weapon to against Blood Betty. He succeeds in weakening her enough that he is able to send her back to The Galactic Bastard's cosmic domain. After this one last act of heroism The Crimson Protector dies.

The Graphic Novel is released but is quickly forgotten on account of the fact that in that year another superhero (published by one of the big two comic companies) also dies (though he gets better). Dicky didn't care because he was proud of the end product no matter what people thought. Shortly afterwards a comic simply titled Kid Crimson is launched to replace The Crimson Protector comic book.

The comic picks up shortly after the after math of the death of The Crimson Protector. Kid Crimson proceeds to join a superhero team made up of members who happen to be the children of member of The LSP. As time goes by the comic becomes more of a team book. Barry Thurston works as artist on the comic until it's cancelation in 1997.

---

38 The scene in question was so controversial that Dicky has said he will not discuss it to this day.

At around the same time Dicky decided to launch a new Freak Squad comic featuring the version in the Death of The Crimson Protector graphic novel. They are joined by former LSP member Frank Mann, the son of Starry Knight. Frank is shown as recently being kicked out of The LSP for getting drunk and crashing American Man's crash. He joins Cross Eyed Mary (Jason Jonze's half Martian daughter), Flesh Column (a man experimented by aliens who looks somewhat like one of Clive Barker's Cenobites dressed as a biker), Krokar (an odd creature with a wizard's hat that can turn into a giant crab/lobster creature), Kat the Catgirl Secretary, Wheelchair Bound leader Tom Hologram and several others. This ends up becoming the most successful version of Freak Squad (it even continues to be published long after WCI's demise).

In 1994 Dicky's son Waldo wanted to work in comics as a writer/ artist. Though nowhere as good as either his mother or uncle, the fourteen year old wanted to work in comics. Even though Dicky feels his son's work isn't publishable he relents and assists in Waldo getting to publish a comic at WCI. Richard had two rules in place for the title. One, Dicky would co-write it with his son and Two if Waldo got behind in his art duties in anyway Dicky would bring in another artist.

Years later Waldo would look back at his art at the time and would cringe. He was trying his hardest to draw like his heroes who worked at Image Comics but he couldn't hold a candle to them (he has even said that he makes Pat Lee' s work look good in comparison). Many would ignore these limitations especially since Waldo had only worked on the first two[39] issues (he would fall back on his obligations shortly after that and would be confined to co-writing the comic and designing new characters). Still people liked that comic.

---

39 And on those two issues Waldo would be heavily inked not looking nearly as bad as the original pencils.

That comic would be called Captain Saltire[40] and The Turbo Task Force. It would star a Scottish WWI veteran who was given superpowers by aliens then frozen until the early nineties and then be turned into a cyborg superhero. He was joined by the Turbo Task Force which consisted of Alvina the robot (whose gigantic robot breasts held her robot brain[41]), Lana the mechanic (possibly the only realistically drawn female in the series), Bigman (a very large individual) and many others.

The series itself would go back and forth between being a tribute to the Grim and Gritty comics of the time (usually Waldo's influence) to being a savage parody of them (usually because of Richard being influenced by the comics of John Wagner and Pat Mills). Some would say this would create a sort of mood whiplash. This would lead to Waldo (who on good days could write almost as good as Brandon Choi while on bad days would write like Hank Kanalz) to write in an "Extreme Nineties Comics" style while Dicky would write in a darkly humorous way.

---

40 Saltire being the name of the Scottish Flag.

41 The robot brain being in Alvina's breast was something Dicky wrote as a joke after he saw her ridiculously large breasts. Waldo didn't get the joke and so it stayed in the comic. Waldo has gone on record recently saying he is embarrassed by the size of Alvina's breasts.

Alvina the robot

Captain Saltire

Captain Saltire

Waldo w Nuevo 94

**Very rough designs of Alvina the Robot and Captain Saltire.
To say the art was subpar would be an understatement.**

The finalized design of Captain Saltire. It just shows how much of a good decision it was to have Waldo Winecrest heavily inked on his issues as artist on the comic. It also shows it was more of a good idea to replace him as artist on the comic.

By 1995 the comic was filled with extreme violence, nudity and sex. This was a result of Dicky pushing the adult content of the book to its limits. This was something that shocked people seeing as it was a collaboration between a father and his teenage son. The comic was graphic even by the standards of the grim and gritty comics of the time.

But the shocking content in the comics were always meant to be for humorous effect and most often some of the most extreme content was suggested by young Waldo. Ironically Waldo was co-writing a comic he could most likely not purchase himself.

Captain Saltire lasted until Waldo went off to college in 1999 (Waldo had to repeat a grade which meant he had not graduated High school until 1999) Dicky decided that this would be the formal ending of WCI. Dicky then canceled The LSP.[42] Dicky would officially closed the doors to the office and decide to go into semi-retirement.

Dicky and Sally moved to Springfield, MO to be closer to Waldo who had been accepted to SMS.[43] Still Dicky would write and self publish Freak Squad until Dec. 2006. After that Dicky would write one last comic (released in 2007) and then decide to not ever write again.

This final project that was self published by Dicky was a Graphic Novel called Once Upon a Time . . . There was Death[44]. The comic based itself was based on a screenplay Dicky had been working on since the eighties. It was meant to be an epic western inspired by films like those directed by Sergio Leone and Sam Peckinpaw.

---

42 By this time The LSP, Freak Squad and Captain Saltire and his Turbo Task Force were the only comics published by WCI.
43 Now MSU.
44 Released in European countries as Once Upon a Time There Were Gunslingers.

The Graphic Novel had been about a man named Alejandro[45] Borges and his revenge for the death of his family. It starts in 1927 with an elderly Alejandro going home after a showing of Fritz Lang's Metropolis is interrupted. He goes home and then is reminded of his youth by the clock his grandfather gave him. He looks back at his youth during the time of the old west. He thinks of the journey he went through to seek revenge. Revenge he sought because of the completely senseless death of his entire family.

During this journey he is accompanied by an elderly Samurai turned Gunslinger[46], the Samurai's apprentice and the apprentice's seven year old daughter. All seek revenge against the blind corrupt landowner and his lackeys who are to blame for all their woes. Blood, death and heartbreak follow the four wherever they go.

When it was released it barely made back the money Dicky had spent to publish it and it was severely savaged by critics. Many felt in some ways was too decompressed in some places while in other places many felt there were too many panels per page. It was considered to have an inconsistent pacing.

Another criticism leveled at the Graphic Novel was that it wasn't realistic. Much is cited about how one character is able to drag Alejandro on his horse from a snow covered forest in Washington State to a ghost town in California. There was also medical related criticism.

For instance many criticized how many characters were able to survive wounds that would surely kill them while others drop off like flies. Another criticism is within a scene in which a character's arm is

---

45 Named after Alejandro Vasquez.
46 Who has a giant scare over his right eye leaving him blind in his right eye.

amputated using a fish deboning knife. Dicky has said he can agree on the pacing but when it comes to the so called unrealistic elements of the comic he says that the critics miss the point.

Dicky would say that, "The whole thing was meant to be an American myth. So things like geography and medical accuracy weren't important to me. It was meant as my love letter to Sergio Leone, Sam Peckinpaw, Akira Kurosawa, Chang Cheh, Kenji Misumi, Sergio Corbucci and a bunch of other stuff.

"It was meant to be both dark and grand. It was a western that was intended to be a gritty epic. It was meant to be a Myth of the West that wasn't hindered by historical, geographical or medical accuracy. It just was what it was."

After the critical and commercial failure of Once Upon a Time ... There was Death led to Dicky abandoning what he was intending as his next project. That project was to be called The Children who Played War. It was intended as a darkly comedic and surreal graphic novel. It was an idea that had been gestating in Dicky's mind for years. It was intended to be his profound statement on war.

Dicky had a completed script but he quickly shelved it after the public reaction to Once Upon a Time ... There was Death. Copies of this script have gotten on the internet. This has made it somewhat infamous. Many were repulsed by the scenes described in the script.

When it had been leaked on the internet many felt that it was too dark. It was infamous for its bleak worldview, and the large amount of graphically violent scenes. Many felt it was a half-assed concept of a once great writer while others felt it was Dicky's lost masterpiece.

It pains me to describe the atrocities found within the script. I have decided to try and describe it in as little detail as possible. I will do this because I am uncomfortable in describing it. This does not necessarily mean I do not like said script but it does disturb me.

The Children who played War is set in a world were very old men in robes send children to fight in a war on a muddy battlefield. As time goes on the innocent children become deranged and sadistic. The turning of the innocent into the deranged is a large aspect of the story. As such the children commit many atrocities throughout the story. To this day Dicky will still not comment on it though he was willing to give me a concept drawing he did.

A concept drawing that Dicky was intending to show his intended artist what he wanted the comic to look like. This is mild compared to what is in the script.

As a result of both the bad reaction of Once Upon a Time ...There was Death and the cancelation of any work on The Children Who played War Dicky decided to go into full retirement mode. He has been in said retirement mode since then. Sally on the other hand still makes children's picture books.

They seem to very much like their lives as they live it at the moment. This includes them usually going out to see Waldo every Tuesday for dinner at the local TGIF Fridays. Waldo is currently busy as a producer at a local TV station in Springfield MO but he is not too busy see his parents.

I myself met Dicky and Sally at a writer's event that I attended. I have been close friends with Dicky and Sally ever since then. A year after I met them I asked them if I could write a book about the history of Weird Comics Incorporated. At first Richard was hesitant while Sally was very interest in having a book be made. Eventually Sally convinced Dicky to say yes. So with that I started interviewing them (as well as anyone else associated with WCI who would want to speak to me).

The book that I proposed to make is the one you are reading right now.

Chapter Notes on Interviews

Chapter 1: I interviewed Dicky Winecrest for this chapter.

Chapter 2: I interviewed Dicky Winecrest and (the late) Phil Hardy.

Chapter 3: I interviewed Dicky Winecrest and Stan Spitz for this chapter.

Chapter 4: For this chapter I interviewed Stan Spitz, Dicky Winecrest and Sally Spitz-Winecrest.

Chapter 5: For this chapter I interviewed Stan Spitz, Dicky Winecrest and Sally Spitz-Winecrest.

Chapter 6: I interviewed Jim Von Bakerson, Stan Spitz, Sally Spitz-Winecrest and Dicky Winecrest for this chapter.

Chapter 7: For this chapter I interviewed Sally Spitz-Winecrest, Dicky Winecrest and Waldo Winecrest.

Review of the Book by Reginald Summerset III

The book that I am about to review which I received in advanced to its publication is one that is a sad state of affairs. It could have been great. It could have been a good look into the history of a much forgotten comic book company but instead it is a failure.

First off the book is littered with Footnotes. They seem to serve no purpose but confuse the reader. Many of the footnotes include information that is present in the main text of the book leading to redundancy throughout the entire book. There also seems to be a bad instance of repetition throughout the book. He just repeats some information over and over. This gets very distracting and annoying. This kind of thing is annoying by the way. On top of this Mr. Webb happens to clutter his book with unimportant information while ignoring that which he should cover.

The late Phil Hardy only gets a minimal amount of space in the book. This is as much a crime as the fact that trailblazer Jim Von Bakerson is only mentioned on a handful of projects talked about in the chapter detailing WCI's publishing in the nineteen eighties. Webb not only ignores many important creators working at WCI he also ignores many comics published by WCI. Surprisingly the many crossovers between Koltar and The Crimson Protector are not mentioned at all while countless comics of varying genres besides superheroes are not mentioned at all.

There are many spelling and grammar problems throughout the whole book. Mr. Webb seems to have never taken anything past the most elementary of composition classes. He is inconsistent with punctuating titles and characters that start with the word the. Sometimes he will capitalize and other times he will not. This just comes off as sloppy on Mr. Webb's part.

Another problem found within the form of the book is that there is a considerably large amount of run on sentences. It's as if Webb feels he is writing a H. P. Lovecraft pastiche as opposed to a document detailing the history of a comic book company. This is not how to write a non-fiction book at all. It comes off like it was the F grade essay of a high school senior. Webb should be ashamed of himself for the complete abomination that he has brought to the world in this book.

Though only a small problem Mr. Webb mixes up the terms Mini-Series and Maxi-Series. He does this when referring to the Mini-Series The Cosmic Turning Point. Webb interchanges the words Maxi-Series and Mini-Series in a way that shows that he is extremely ignorant of the meaning of either word. This creates a sense that Webb is a man that seems to live in a world in which he is protected from editors.

Speaking of protection from editors there is a small portion in Chapter 4 that any editor worth their salt would have had deleted from the text. In this portion of the book Sally Spitz-Winecrest talks about how Dicky Winecrest did not want to get married because he thought marriage might shackle Sally. This comes out of nowhere and then is quickly forgotten. On top of that it's a very personal matter that does not fit properly in the book. Yet said section remains in the book sticking out like a sore thumb. But this is a minor issue when compared to Webb's deplorable sentence structure and bad grammar.

It is a shame that on top of all this Mr. Webb decided to only rely on original research. The fact he didn't attempt to either quote or paraphrase from previous interviews is a shame. It shows nothing more than his utter contempt for the previous work of others who have examined the history of WCI.

There are many instances of interviews previously done by others that Mr. Webb could have used for reference. Many of these interviews were made with many who have been involved with WCI (including Dicky Winecrest). And Yet Mr. Webb has decided to ignore these interviews for original research.

The most egregiously is the fact he has ignored all interviews made with the late Richard Winecrest. The fact that these were not used in the book is a travesty. Sure I did interview Richard Winecrest in a fanzine and yes I felt it should have been included in this book but that is beside the point.

On top of all this the book is one of the shortest books on the subject of Sequential Art I have ever read. Again there was a lot of important history that Webb did not delve into in any meaningful way. There are countless Creators and creations clearly forgotten by Mr. Webb.

Maybe I care too much. But I can't sit by and let this book go unnoticed for the problems that are entangled within its pages. Another problem with this book is the fact that there are many asinine chapter titles. That while some make sense others seem like complete gibberish. This definitely comes off amateurish and the fault of a first time writer. No I take that back, a first time writer would know not to come up with such stupid chapter titles. It really comes off like the chapter titles were written by a crack addicted monkey on ADHD.

His use of repetition for no reason is annoying and distracting. It serves no purpose at all. It is a crime I say. A crime I say. This is something that should not be prevalent in a book about the beloved comic book company Weird Comics Incorporated.

Some might say I'm being too harsh with this author. Some might say that I wrote this in haste and without an editor. Some might say I am committing some of the same things in this review that I condemn Mr. Webb for. Some might say I start too many sentences with the words "On top" or "On top of that" which Mr. Webb also does. Some might say that when I compared Mr. Webb to a crack addicted monkey on ADHD I was being cruel. Some may say I am being too harsh. I honestly think I'm not being harsh enough. I feel that I have pulled my punches. I feel that I had to get this off my chest. I feel I had to show my full contempt for this book.

In the end the point of this review is to point out that the book Simply Weird is a sad excuse for a book. It is a travesty and a shame to the name of Weird Comics Incorporated. I feel I have not emphasized this enough. If there is a better book to be made from the history of WCI then most likely I will have to write it.

Author's reaction to Reginald Summerset III's Review

First off I find the reference to a crack addicted monkey on ADHD to be in poor taste. This hits me as a harsh criticism especially in light of the fact that I do have ADHD and . . . oh Shiny . . . [47]

I agree with some of what you have said. Some things I obviously don't agree with on. But I find it ironic that a man writes a review that comes off more like a rant than a professional review. Now I understand that your emotions got ahead of you. You probably didn't even have your editor look over it.

I'll admit I have some idiosyncrasies within my writing but not more than you do. I could berate you for your own idiosyncrasies but I won't. That's your style and I have my style.

As for you writing a book to examine the things I didn't cover in my book well I would love to read that book. I would love to find out what you could come up with. I will admit that my book dealt with a very small portion of WCI's History but that is the book I set out to write. You cannot fault me for that.

Maybe I'm being an asshole and your right. Maybe my work is shit. I don't know. This was my first book and all. But I hope that if anything comes from this book is my undying passion for the medium of comics and I can tell you yourself have a similar passion for the medium.

---

47 Just kidding about the Oh Shiny part. But seriously I do have ADHD and I do find your reference to ADHD in your review to be in poor taste.

We have such a passion for the medium. As such we shouldn't be fighting. We should embrace our common attributes and become friends.

Still I want to ask you one thing. It's something that I honestly want to know. Can't we just be friends?

Reginald Summerset III's reaction to Mr. Webb's Reaction

What?

Mr. Webb's Last Reaction

You are welcome . . .